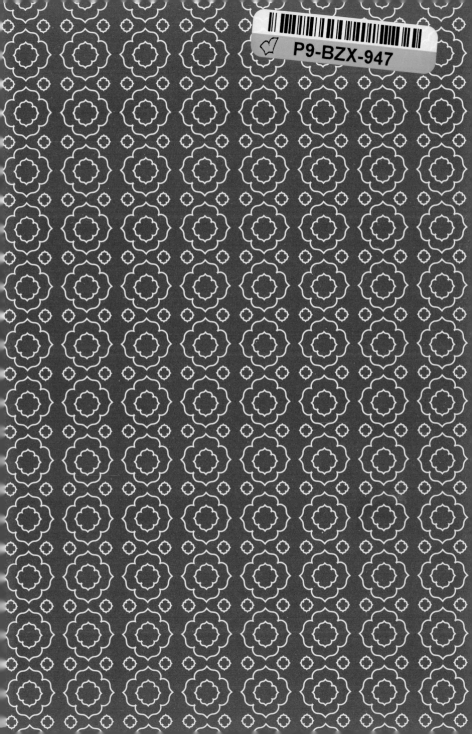

Emma and the Blue Genie

CORNELIA FUNKE

TRANSLATED BY OLIVER LATSCH

ILLUSTRATED BY KERSTIN MEYER

RANDOM HOUSE 🏠 NEW YORK

For Kerstin Meyer,
and for Anna and Ben,
who came along for the entire journey on the carpet.
Oh yes, and for Luna as well, of course,
even though she doesn't look anything like Tristan.

Text copyright © 2002 by Cornelia Funke
Translation copyright © 2014 by Oliver Latsch
Cover art copyright © 2014 by Vivienne To
Interior illustrations copyright © 2014 by Kerstin Meyer

All rights reserved. Published in the United States by Random House Children's Books, a division of Random House LLC, a Penguin Random House Company, New York. Originally published as *Emma und der Blaue Dschinn* by Cecilie Dressler Verlag GmbH & Co. KG, Hamburg, Germany, in 2002.

Random House and the colophon are registered trademarks of Random House LLC.

Visit us on the Web! randomhouse.com/kids

Educators and librarians, for a variety of teaching tools, visit us at RHTeachersLibrarians.com

Library of Congress Cataloging-in-Publication Data
Funke, Cornelia Caroline.
[Emma und der Blaue Dschinn. English]
Emma and the blue genie / Cornelia Funke ; translated by Oliver Latsch ; illustrated by Kerstin Meyer. — First American edition.
pages cm.
"Originally published as Emma und der Blaue Dschinn by Cecilie Dressler Verlag GmbH & Co. KG, Hamburg, Germany, in 2002."
Summary: Eight-year-old Emma and her little dog, Tristan, take a magic carpet ride to the distant land of Barakash to help a genie recover his stolen magical nose ring.
ISBN 978-0-385-37540-5 (trade) — ISBN 978-0-385-37542-9 (lib. bdg.) — ISBN 978-0-385-37543-6 (ebook)
[1. Genies — Fiction. 2. Magic — Fiction. 3. Adventure and adventurers — Fiction. 4. Dogs — Fiction.] I. Latsch, Oliver, translator. II. Meyer, Kerstin, illustrator. III. Title.
PZ7.F96624Emm 2014 [Fic] — dc23 2013029268

MANUFACTURED IN CHINA

10 9 8 7 6 5 4 3 2 1

CONTENTS

1

THE BOTTLE IN THE MOONLIGHT

Emma loved the ocean. The house where she and her family lived stood right behind the dunes, and at night you could hear the waves rush over the sand. To Emma that was the most beautiful lullaby in the world. Her four brothers, however, thought that it sounded like a growling sea monster, and it made them dream of giant octopuses that pulled them out of their beds with wet arms.

Brothers are strange. During the day they fight and scuffle, and at night their fear of the dark won't let them sleep. Nearly every night

one of Emma's brothers crawled into her bed to hide from sea monsters and octopuses, only to immediately start snoring so noisily that she couldn't hear the rush of the sea anymore.

It was on nights like those that Emma put on her bathrobe and snuck out of the house to trudge through the dark and down to the water.

The salty wind whispering across the waves, the beach stretching from one end of the night to the other, it all belonged to her alone. It was wonderful. Four brothers can be quite hard work for one girl, so every now and then she really needed a little solitude.

The darkness never scared Emma. After all, she had Tristan with her. His legs might have been as short as bratwursts, and his tail might have looked like a twirly noodle, but he also had lots of pointy teeth in his mouth.

Sitting on wet sand is not very comfortable, so Emma always took a cushion with her to the beach. On that cushion Emma and Tristan sat side by side, and the sea breathed at their feet like a living thing.

On clear nights, when the moon poured a silver highway onto the water, Emma imagined that at the other end of that highway lay the most beautiful and wondrous land on earth. People rode on camels, and palm trees swayed in the warm breeze. There were no brothers in that land, or maybe a few teeny-weeny ones who were very gentle and only wanted to scuffle on Saturdays. Nobody went to school or had to work. The sun shone every day, and there was just enough rain to water the oases, which lay like shimmering diamonds at the edge of the desert.

Who knows?

Maybe the moon likes to eavesdrop on the thoughts of girls who sit alone by the sea with noodle-tailed dogs. Maybe he listens to their dreams and tries to make them come true. Maybe . . .

One night, when Emma again came trudging down the beach with Tristan and their cushion, there was a bottle floating in the moon-silvered water. It bobbed just a few steps away from the water's edge. It shimmered and flickered as though someone had stuffed it with a thousand glowworms. Emma tried to pull the bottle from the water, but her arms were at least a couple of feet too short. So Tristan waded into the cold waves.

"I wonder what's in there," Emma said, as Tristan dropped the bottle in front of her feet. "Do you think I should open it?"

The glimmering and glowing made her feel a little uneasy, but Tristan just looked at her and smacked his lips, which meant something like, "Of course you should open it!" If he'd meant, "You better not!" he would have turned his backside to her.

"Fine. If you say so," Emma said. "But it's your fault if something bad happens." Then she pulled the stopper from the bottle.

2

KARIM

Cornflower-blue smoke billowed from the bottle. More and more of it. Emma stumbled back, and Tristan stuck his head in the sand. The blue smoke grew arms and legs and a head so bald and shiny that it reflected the moonlight.

"Sssaaalaaaaam aalaaaikum!" the ghost from the bottle whispered. "Greeeeetings, oh my fair savior! My name is Karim, Karim the Beardless." And he bowed so deeply that his bald head touched the sand.

"Very ... pleased to meet you!" Emma stammered. She also bowed (though not quite so deeply). When she straightened herself up again, she noticed that the genie was only a head taller than her.

"I am sorry," Emma said (after all, she didn't know whether genies were easily offended), "but are you still growing? I mean, as far as I remember, the genies in my fairy tales are always huge."

Karim sighed so deeply that the sand stirred up and covered his naked toes. "Ooh, you are *so* right, my mistress!" he called out dolefully. "And I once was indeed much bigger. I could shake the hand of my caliph while he stood on the highest tower of his palace. His dromedary would sleep in the palm of my hand. Yet now I am as small as a desert hedgehog and as weak as a nosebug." With these words, the genie began to sob so hard that his tears dropped on the sand like rain.

"Oh dear!" Emma said comfortingly. "And how did you become so small?"

Tristan pulled his head out of the sand and

sniffed Karim's toes, which Emma thought was not very respectful.

"Can't you see?" the genie sniveled. "My nose ring is gone! Stolen in a heinous act of treachery. Without the ring I am nothing—a maggot, a mere mouse, a snail being scorched and shriveled by the sun."

"Ah!" Emma exclaimed. She looked at Karim's blue nose. It did look rather naked. "Who stole the ring?" she asked.

Karim rubbed his hand over his eyes. "Sahim!" he breathed. "Sahim, the Master of Evil. The most dastardly of all yellow genies. He stole my ring, he stuffed me into that bottle, and he threw me into the sea."

"Hmm . . . ," Emma murmured. She dug the tip of her shoe into the sand. "So I guess I'm not getting my three wishes? I mean . . . those three wishes all the fairy tales always talk about. You know, the wishes you get when you free a genie?"

Karim shook his head glumly. "Without the ring, I can't grant you even the tiniest, bug-sized wish, my mistress!" he said. "You should just throw me back into the ocean so that I can drown myself in my tears!" And he started to sob again.

Emma quickly held out a handkerchief. It was a bit crumpled and smelled of dog biscuits, but the genie accepted it gladly.

"That's really not a reason to cry," said Emma, while Karim dabbed the tears from his lashes (and even his lashes were blue, by the way). "I wouldn't have known what to wish for anyway."

"You are too generous, my mistress!" the genie sniffed. He smiled sadly as he handed

Emma her handkerchief. "I shall be in your debt forever and three thousand days."

He leaned down and picked up his bottle. He shook it and something dropped out of it, something that looked like a crumpled piece of fabric. Yet when the genie gently blew on it, the cloth started to unfurl like a flower, and it was suddenly a carpet. It looked a little tattered, but it was very, very beautiful.

The genie shuddered as he shook the cold, damp sand from his feet; then he sat down on the carpet with a deep sigh. "Farewell, my mistress!" he said with a quaver in his voice. "I shall fly back to my homeland to free my caliph and all of Barakash from the yellow genie. But you have Karim's solemn vow: I shall return as soon as my ring is back on this wretched nose. By then you will definitely have thought of three wishes."

He clapped his hands, and the carpet rose and carried him out over the sea.

Emma stood there and looked after the genie. She had no idea why she was suddenly so sad. The wind blew her hair into her eyes, and Karim's figure slowly melted into the darkness. "Oh, Tristan, I hope he really does come back," she said. "Not because of the wishes. Really. I mean, yes, I definitely could have thought of some. But I would like to hear more about that yellow genie."

Tristan shoved his nose against her knee. He looked up at her expectantly.

"Of course!" Emma called. "Why didn't I think of that? Karim! Karim, wait! Tristan says we're coming with you!"

The night had already all but swallowed Karim's blue figure, and at first Emma thought he hadn't heard her. But then she saw the carpet flying back toward the beach.

"Yallah!" the genie shouted. He pulled at the carpet's tassels, but still crashed down so hard next to Emma that he rolled headfirst into the sand. "Apologies, but I am a little out of practice!" he huffed as he stood up. "Did I hear you right? You want to accompany me? That is . . . ahem . . . certainly an honor, but . . ." Karim cleared his throat and lowered his voice. "You are still very young," he whispered to Emma, "and your dog is barely bigger than a desert rat. How is he going to challenge the Master of Evil?

Either he has the heart of a lion, or his mind is a little weak."

"Oh, his mind is perfectly fine," Emma said a little crossly, "and believe me, we are used to trouble. I have four brothers, and Tristan has to deal with dogs twice his size all the time. So I don't think he's going to be scared by some yellow genie."

Tristan seemed to agree, for he strutted toward the carpet, gave it a little sniff, and then rolled himself up on it.

Karim looked at Tristan as though he'd never seen a dog. "By the beardless chin of my caliph!" he shouted. "Dogs are not valued very highly in Barakash, but from this day on I shall bow my head in respect to every one of them."

"Good. That's settled then," said Emma.

Before they took off, Emma quickly wrote a note to her parents:

Don't worry. I'm off with a pretty big genie to find his nose ring. And I have Tristan with me. Love, Emma

The "pretty big" was of course an exaggeration, but Emma felt it made the whole thing sound a little less worrisome.

"How far is it to your caliph?" she asked Karim as they flew out over the ocean.

"You will see his palace at sunrise," the genie answered.

"Ah!" Emma sighed. She just realized she was still wearing her bathrobe. That was a little embarrassing, since she was flying to see a genuine caliph.

Tristan didn't have to worry about such things. He had already tucked his nose under his tail and was sleeping soundly.

But Emma didn't want to sleep. After all, this was the most exciting night of her life (and being eight years old, she'd already lived through nearly three thousand nights!).

But then, over some strange ocean, her eyes fell shut.

3

THE PALACE OF WILTED FLOWERS

When Emma opened her eyes again, she saw a bright red sun hanging above a very, very strange-looking country. There were palm trees and towers and domes and white houses stuck together like a giant honeycomb.

"Oh, Barakash! So I finally see you again!" Karim crooned. He wiped a tear from his nose. Then he began to dissolve into blue smoke. "My return should remain a secret for now!" he whispered to Emma. "You should land in front of the palace. The palace is right behind those palm trees there." And with that he disappeared into his bottle.

"Land? What are you talking about?" Emma cried out. The tassels of the carpet only barely missed snagging on a spire. "Karim!" she hissed into the bottle. "Come back! I can't do this."

"Pull the tassels and call 'yallah!'" the genie whispered. "The carpet usually obeys quite well."

And truly, after Emma had pulled three tassels of the fringe and had shouted "yallah!" five times, the carpet landed as lightly as a feather in front of the caliph's palace. The streets and alleys lay deserted. Only an old woman was dragging her donkey across the square. The sight of a flying carpet did not seem to surprise her at all.

"And what now?" Emma whispered into the bottle. Tristan jumped off the carpet and made straight for the next palm tree to lift his leg.

"This may feel a little wet!" the genie whispered.

And before Emma could ask him exactly what he meant, it had already happened. "Yuck!" she hissed angrily. "Did you just spit in my ear?"

"Forgive me, my mistress!" the genie whispered. "But now you can understand our language. Go to the guard by the main entrance and tell him you have a message for Maimun, the caliph of Barakash. You must insist that you can deliver it only to Maimun in person."

Emma did as he said, though she was still angry about the spitting. She tucked Karim's bottle into her bathrobe and rolled up the flying carpet before waving Tristan to her. The dog had been giving the palace wall a good sniff. Her heart beating wildly, Emma went to the gate.

The guard had a giant scimitar, he wore the tallest turban Emma had ever seen, and he looked quite cranky.

"Excuse me," Emma said. She tried to look as dignified as possible (which wasn't very easy in a bathrobe). "I have an urgent message for Maimun, the caliph of Barakash."

"And what is that message, you little flea?" the guard asked. He ran a thumb along the blade of his hideous saber.

"The message is from Karim, the most powerful of the blue genies," Emma answered. "And I can deliver it only to the caliph himself."

"Karim?" the guard grunted. "He's gone. There's only one genie in Barakash now, and that is Sahim the Insatiable."

"Really?" Emma replied. "If you don't bring me to the caliph right away, Karim will put a knot in your saber. Then you'll see that he's not gone."

"Will you listen to that!" the guard growled. He leaned down toward Emma and smiled, exposing five and a half gold teeth. "Listen, you obnoxious daughter of a sandmite!" he whispered into Emma's ear. "All of Barakash would rejoice if Karim returned, but nobody has seen him in more than a hundred days."

"I have," said Emma.

The guard again smiled his shiny, gold-toothed smile. Then he called a servant who was so big that Tristan could have completely disappeared in his slippers. Without giving Emma a glance, the servant opened the gate and led her into the palace.

Emma had never been in a palace before. Where she came from didn't have too many palaces. But she was sure there couldn't have been a palace more beautiful than this one anywhere in the world.

Sadly, Tristan didn't seem to notice any of this. Emma had to constantly stop him from peeing on the pillars.

Yes, the palace of the caliph of Barakash was indeed beautiful. But it felt as if sadness itself lived there. All the servants Emma saw kept their heads bowed low. There were no smiles on their faces, and as they walked through the

gardens, Tristan's paws sank deeply into a layer of wilted flowers. "Sahim dried up all our wells!" the huge servant whispered to Emma. "He hates water, because it is cool and because it reflects the blue sky. Yellow genies hate everything that is blue and everything that is cooler than their hot yellow skin. They even hate the night, because it is cold and makes them stiff. That's why

Sahim only comes at midday, when it is so hot that even the lizards hide in the shade, and when the air you breathe burns your tongue."

"Does he come every day?" Emma asked with worry.

The servant shook his head. "Sometimes we don't see him for several days," he whispered. "But he sends his scorpions. They are his eyes. They used to hunt only during the night, but Sahim taught them to love the burning sun as much as he does."

"Scorpions?" Emma asked. She nearly stumbled over Tristan, who had again lifted his leg next to a pillar.

"Shhh!" the servant hissed as he put his finger to his lips. Emma looked around, but all she saw were two lizards that looked nothing like scorpions.

"And when Sahim comes himself?" Emma whispered. "What happens then?"

"The Master of Evil has many demands!" the servant whispered back. He had stopped in front of a door that was so tall even he could barely reach the handle. "The last time he took all of the caliph's tame golden flamingos, and he commanded that everything blue in the palace be burned. Even though the caliph's dromedary loves nothing better than blue grapes. Oh, it is terrible!" And with a deep, very deep sigh, he opened the massive door.

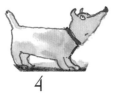

4

NO FRIENDLY WELCOME

The throne of the caliph of Barakash looked like the lounge chair of a giant. Yet sitting on top of the gold-embroidered cushions was a boy barely older than Emma. His feet rested on the hump of a honey-golden dromedary that lay on its knees in front of the throne, chewing on something in a rather halfhearted way. Lounging on a sumptuous cushion next to the dromedary was a big woman with a beard and blue patterns on her face. She was sipping tea from a cup.

Emma would have loved to take a closer look at the dromedary, but the servant (who was called Hashim, by the way) threw himself flat on the ground and made frantic signals for Emma to do the same.

"Forgive me, oh Maimun, most exalted

navel of the world!" he called without taking his nose off the floor tiles. "Forgive me for disturbing you and your honorable grandmother at such an early hour. But this strangely clad girl claims she is bearing a message from Karim."

"Karim?"

The caliph leaned forward on his throne to give Emma a curious look.

"Leave us alone!" the caliph ordered the servant, who immediately backed away with a thousand curtsies.

"Could I maybe get up, please?" Emma asked. The stone tiles had a beautiful pattern, but they were horribly cold.

The caliph frowned—and nodded. "You shall be permitted," he said. "Where do you

come from? You look strange, as though you fell into a sack of flour."

"Where I come from a lot of people look like this," Emma answered. She wasn't sure whether she should feel insulted or not.

"Really?" Maimun said. He brushed a jet-black strand of hair from his forehead. "I've heard stories about places like that, but I've always thought them to be fairy tales." Then he shot a frown at Tristan, who had started growling at the dromedary. "Girls and dogs are usually forbidden from entering the palace," Maimun observed. "If your dog bites my dromedary, I'll have to throw him into the dungeon."

"He never bites," Emma said, as she pulled Tristan back by his tail. "He just likes to act dangerous. Now, do you want to hear my message or not?" She was losing patience with the caliph and had already decided not to like him, no matter what Karim thought about him.

Maimun, however, crossed his arms and gave Emma a scornful look. "If your message really is from Karim," he said, "then it is the message of a traitor. Karim abandoned Barakash! He ran from Sahim like a dog from a lion."

"My dog would never run from a lion!" Emma shouted. "And Karim didn't run away, either. You should be ashamed for even thinking that of him." She pulled the green bottle from under her bathrobe and put it on the floor.

A pale-blue Karim drifted out of the neck of the bottle. He took shape and bowed to the caliph, his patterned grandmother, and the dromedary.

"Karim!" Maimun called out. His eyes went so wide that his eyebrows disappeared under the edge of his turban. Emma was just wondering how Maimun got down from his enormous throne, when he skipped onto his dromedary's hump and slid to the floor.

"Where have you been, Karim?" Maimun

cried, running toward the genie. "Sahim dried out all our wells. He stole my flamingos and my Barbary sheep, and he dragged all my treasure into his palace. My subjects, my grandmother, my dromedary, even I—all of Barakash has nothing to eat but dried bread. And still Sahim keeps coming with new demands. Oh, Karim!" He flung his arms around the genie's neck. "How could you abandon us like that? Every day I called your name a hundred times, but you never came!"

"Well, now he's here!" the blue-patterned grandmother said as she rose from her pillows. "But look at him! He's as pale as diluted grape juice and as thin as a carpet tassel."

Karim cast a sad look down at himself. "I am not to blame for my pitiful condition, oh grandmother of the greatest of all caliphs!" he said. "Sahim's scorpions stole my nose ring while I was sleeping. You know that we blue genies sleep at midday, when the sun makes even the stones sweat."

"Ah yes, the midday nap of the blue genies!" Maimun's grandmother grimaced. "Such careless folly, since every child knows that the midday hour belongs to the yellow genies and that they use their time for nothing but evil."

"Well, it happened!" Karim retorted testily. "And the sea lurched me back and forth for more than a hundred days and a hundred nights, until this pale flower of a frigid land"—he bowed so deeply to Emma that she blushed—"freed me from my glassy prison. She selflessly turned

her back on her home to join me with her black-nosed friend so that together we may retrieve my ring. So be it, or may my name no longer be Karim the Beardless!"

Maimun (who really wasn't much bigger than Emma, either) eyed Emma and Tristan with incredulous respect. His grandmother, however, didn't seem too impressed by Karim's report.

"Hear, hear!" she grumbled, which Emma didn't think was very polite at all. "And how are you lot going to do that? Sahim is, after all, the most powerful of the yellow genies."

"Well, Karim is the mightiest of the blue genies, Grandmother!" Maimun called out.

"Even if he doesn't really look like it at the moment," Karim added. He tried to puff himself up a little, but he only managed to grow a pathetic two and a half inches. The dromedary grunted its contempt and spat a couple of pomegranate seeds onto the throne.

"What about Sahim's spiders?" the blue-patterned grandmother asked. She shoved a banana between the dromedary's yellow teeth. "They are as snappish as desert cats! And his scorpions—"

Karim interrupted her impatiently. "Their venom can't harm a genie!"

"What spiders?" Emma asked uneasily. But nobody paid any attention to her. Only the dromedary's sleepy eyes watched her and Tristan.

"You just keep talking, you pale shadow of a genie!" the blue-patterned grandmother barked at Karim. "Yet I tell you, you are crazy if you think you can take the ring from Sahim's palace with nobody but a flour-faced girl and her sausage-legged dog for help!"

Emma was just about to say something very unfriendly to the big old lady, when the guard came storming into the chamber. He dropped to the ground ten steps from the throne and dragged himself a little farther along the cold stone tiles before coming to a halt in front of the first step. "He's coming!" he panted. "He's coming, oh jewel of Barakash!"

That same instant, a scorching-hot wind blew into the chamber, and Karim disappeared into his bottle faster than anyone could have whispered his name.

5

THE YELLOW GENIE

Mustard-yellow smoke billowed into the throne room. It rose right up to the golden ceiling, and the air got so hot that Emma began to feel like a crumpet in an oven. At first there were just two hideous amber-yellow eyes staring out of the swirling mist. Then the smoke solidified into arms and legs, a massive belly, and a head with lips, on which sat the nastiest smile Emma had ever seen. "Greeeetiings, Maimun!" Sahim thundered as he drifted under the ceiling like a giant sulfur cloud. "Did you miss me?"

Maimun called back, "Yes, like a mosquito's sting. Like an abscess. I missed you like I'd miss the bite of a snake!" He tried to sound brave, but his trembling voice gave him away. "What are you doing here again? We have nothing left for you. Absolutely nothing."

"Haaa!" the yellow genie roared. "I'll find something, believe me."

The dromedary stuck its yellow head out from under the throne. Its tail twitched nervously.

Sahim looked around disapprovingly. "There really doesn't seem to be much left to take,

little caliph! Your throne is too uncomfortable for me, your rugs are all already in my palace, your date preserves sweeten my days, your sand larks sing me to sleep, and you can keep your patterned and eternally grumpy grandmother. However . . ."

Emma's knees went as soft as melting butter as Sahim's cat eyes fixed on her.

"What is that girl there?" the yellow genie boomed. "By all the grains of sand in the desert! The little thing is as pale as the belly of a scorpion. Is she always that pale, or did the sight of me make her so?" Sahim put his finger under Emma's chin. "And that yellow hair. Ahhh!" The genie leaned in so close that his breath made Emma's cheeks go red. "You know, little caliph, I love everything yellow, and truly I have never seen a girl with yellow hair. I think I've decided what I'll take today."

Tristan poked his head out from under Emma's bathrobe and let out a deep growl. Emma quickly gave him a warning nudge with her foot. Who knew what a yellow genie might do to a noodle-tailed dog that growled at him?

But Sahim just laughed. He laughed so loudly that the pillars all around them trembled, and the dromedary crept so far under the throne that its hump got stuck. "Yesss, give me the girl, little caliph!" Sahim thundered. He ballooned until he nearly filled the whole hall with his toxic yellow body. "I wanted to take your dromedary today, but I like the girl better. And I'll take the dwarf dog as well. Nobody has dared to growl at me like that in more than three hundred years."

Emma's heart nearly stopped. Sweat dripped off the tip of her nose, and her fear felt like a stone in her throat, but this was too much. "Never!" she screeched at his horrible eyes. "Who do you think you are, you stinky blob of smoke? That is *my* dog!"

"Noooo, Sandy Head. Now he's miiiine!" Sahim howled. "Just like you!" And his giant fingers reached for Tristan's noodle tail, but the dog spun around and dashed off as though he had eight legs and not just four.

"Yes! Run, Tristan! Run!" Emma screamed.

But Sahim laughed again. Then he shook himself like a wet dog, and from his turban poured scores of pincer-snapping scorpions and ink-black spiders. The spiders wrapped Emma up like a silkworm, and the scorpions, their tails raised menacingly, herded Tristan back to their master.

"Sahim, let them go!" Maimun called out. "They are my guests, and they are under my

protection. I will give you my last barrel of honeyed dates for them."

"Your protection? Hahahaaaa! You can't protect anyone. Not even your own city. Come and get your guests, if you can!" Sahim boomed, while the scorpions and the spiders crawled back into his turban. "I'll fetch those dates an-other time—together with your dromedary." And before Emma could free herself from the disgustingly sticky spider threads, the yellow genie grabbed her and Tristan with his scalding-hot fingers and whirled them both off.

6

THE PALACE BENEATH THE SAND

Sahim flew so fast that Emma could barely breathe. His fingers burnt her neck, and Tristan's ears were nearly blown off. Barakash had long vanished beyond the horizon. An endless sea of sand stretched beneath them, and Sahim's shadow flitted across the dunes like a giant thundercloud. But then the yellow genie slowed his flight. He dove down toward a group of rocks that stuck rather forlornly out of the sand and landed between them with a big thud.

"You've gotten even paler!" Sahim breathed into Emma's face. "Did you not like the flight, my little golden bug?" Then he took a deep breath; when his cheeks ballooned like melons, he blew into the sand. The tiny grains flurried up, until they even covered the sun. They burned in Emma's eyes and clogged up her ears. Tristan snapped at them and got a mouthful of crunchy sand. And when the yellow clouds finally sank back, there stood a crumbling palace. Sand poured out of its windows and covered its walls like the icing on a cake. The entrance was so tall that Sahim barely had to duck his head to float through. The inside was as hot as the heart of a fire and as dark as if no beam of sunlight ever entered. But the yellow genie spread so much light that Emma could easily make out all the piles of gold and precious stones Sahim had amassed in his long and evil life.

There was treasure everywhere, in the halls and chambers, even in the corridors Emma and Tristan got dragged along. Sahim blew into the darkness, and a thousand torches flared up. Golden cages hung from a soot-black ceiling. From behind the bars came whistles, hisses, and growls. And before Emma could realize what was happening, she and Tristan had also been stuffed into one of the cages.

"Ahhh!" the yellow genie warbled as he peered through the bars with his cat eyes. "Yes, you are an excellent addition to my collection. And as for your dog, my servants may have to roll him in turmeric powder!"

Tristan barked and snapped at Sahim's nose, but he just stubbed his snout on the cage bars. The yellow genie laughed so loudly that sand came raining down from the palace ceiling.

Then he drifted to an enormous spiderweb that stretched like a hammock from one end of the hall to the other. Sahim sank into it with a deep sigh. "Servants! Bring me honeyed dates!"

he yelled. From the darkness emerged two pale
spirits. They were of a faint yellow color, like
slices of lemon cut too thin, and they were tee-
tering under the weight of a bowl the size of a
bathtub. With constant bows, they set the bowl
on Sahim's naked belly.

The sight made Emma's stomach rumble.

She hadn't eaten anything since before she'd found Karim's bottle on the beach. But then she had a terrifying thought. "Do you also dip your prisoners in honey and eat them?" she called out with a trembling voice to the hungry genie.

Sahim grabbed one of his servants and used him to wipe some honey off his chin. His fanged teeth glistened in the torchlight. "Nonsense,"

he grunted. "They don't taste nice. I just collect them because they are yellow. And their fear gives me strength. Yellow genies love the smell of fear; there is no better scent. And now I want to sleep, so be quiet, or I'll stuff your mouth with sand." Sahim sank back with a burp and immediately started snoring.

Emma felt her fear drowning in rage like a fly in the sea. She rattled the cage and screamed, "Let me out of here right now! Just you wait until Karim gets here. He'll put you in a bottle, and you know what I will do then? I'll spit in it—that's what!"

Suddenly all the other cages fell silent. Hundreds of pairs of eyes were fixed on Emma.

"Karim?" With a growl that sounded like a hungry lion, Sahim sat up in his hammock. "What do you, little slug, know of Karim? There no longer is any Karim. I threw him into the sea. Do you want to see his nose ring?" Sahim flicked his finger against the ring hanging from his oversized earlobe. "There it is. Looks good on me, doesn't it? And now let me sleep, or I'll dip you and your dog in honey after all!"

The genie turned away with an angry grunt and started snoring again. The spiders came crawling out of his turban and began to mend the threads of the web that had torn under Sahim's weight.

The golden cages were oozing despair.

"You do believe that Karim will come to rescue us, right?" Emma whispered to Tristan.

He licked her nose — definitely an encouraging answer.

"Then everything's fine," she mumbled, and dug her face into his back. But sleeping in a cage wasn't easy, even if it was a golden one.

7

A COOL WIND

It turned out to be a horrible night. (Even more
horrible than when one of Emma's brothers had
poured dishwashing soap into her nose.) Tristan
slept as though he was in the most peaceful
place on earth, but Emma couldn't keep her
eyes closed. *I shouldn't have opened that bottle!* she
thought at least three hundred and thirty-five
times while she stared into the darkness. The

yellow genie snored so loudly that her ears began to hurt. A new day dawned, but the only sign of that was a few stray rays of sunshine trickling through the old walls and onto Sahim's nose.

After his breakfast, which consisted of countless little fragrant cakes, the yellow genie set off to pay a visit to Barakash's neighboring kingdom. His pale servants dusted the treasure with peacock feathers and threw dry bread into the cages.

Most of the animals in Sahim's collection were ones Emma had never seen before. But there were also sand-colored foxes with bat-like ears, lizards with spikes on their tails, and long-necked flamingos that poked their beaks through the bars.

Emma wondered how long they'd been here. With every hour she spent in her awful cage, her hope that Karim would come to rescue her shrank a little more. And when Sahim returned that evening to drop into his spiderweb, that hope was barely as big as a pea. A very, very small pea.

The yellow genie devoured a sack of pomegranates and thirteen cinnamon cakes before going to sleep. The torches died one by one, until Sahim's pale-yellow belly was the only thing glowing in the dark. And Emma felt a tear run down her cheek.

"Oh, Tristan! I don't think Karim will come!" she whispered. "Would you mind cheering me up a bit? You could lick that tear off my cheek, maybe?"

But Tristan just lifted his head.

A cool breeze brushed over Emma's face. It drifted so cool and damp through the old palace that Sahim shuddered in his sleep and tossed and turned on his hammock.

"Karim?" Emma breathed.

"Shhh!" came the reply. And a heartbeat later, Karim's flying carpet appeared from the darkness. Kneeling next to the blue genie were Maimun and the dromedary.

"My mistress, forgive us for coming only now!" Karim whispered. "But this palace wasn't easy to find! Luckily the forever-hungry dromedary has a fine nose!"

The dromedary snorted and cast a bored glance around the hall.

Maimun pulled a bunch of keys from his gold-embroidered cloak. "This time Sahim really went too far!" he whispered, while he unlocked Emma's cage with trembling hands. "Capturing my guests! Does he think I'll let him get away with everything? You look even paler than before, oh flower of a cold land!"

"Where did you get the keys?" Emma whispered. As she stepped on the carpet, she decided she did like Maimun after all.

"We took them off two fellows who looked even paler than you," Maimun answered quietly.

"We stuffed them into Karim's bottle. But they didn't have his nose ring."

"Of course not!" Emma whispered back. "Because Sahim is wearing it as an earring!"

Maimun cast a worried look at the yellow genie. Karim, however, seemed so angry that his color changed until his bald head looked like a very ripe blue grape.

"My nose ring on his . . . ear?" he growled. "How dare he, that son of a slimy snail, of a tail-less dog? Oh, forgive me"—Karim bowed to Tristan—"forgive me, king of all dogs. That just slipped out."

Tristan smacked his lips and sniffed the dromedary's backside.

Karim drifted silently into the air. "Wait here," he breathed. And before Maimun or Emma realized what he was doing, he was already drifting, like a pale-blue balloon, toward Sahim's spiderweb hammock.

Karim looked so ridiculously small compared

to the yellow genie that Emma's fear nearly made her forget to breathe.

Sahim snorted in his sleep, and he rubbed his fat belly. Fifteen black spiders were sitting on it.

"Please keep sleeping, you monster," Emma whispered. "Please!"

Nothing moved in the other cages. All of the yellow genie's prisoners seemed to be fast asleep. Only one of the flamingos pulled its head out from under its wing and stared at the flying carpet.

Karim was now only an arm's length from Sahim's mustard-yellow earlobe.

"Oh, please hurry, Karim!" Emma heard Maimun mutter.

Something rustled beneath them. The flamingo had pushed its beak through the bars.

"Maimun! Didn't you say Sahim stole your tame flamingos?" Emma whispered. "Is that one of them over there?"

"Where?" Maimun asked. He turned around.

The bird with the crooked beak let out a bloodcurdling screech of joy as it recognized its former master. The Barbary sheep lifted their heads and began to bleat. The gold jackals barked, and the desert monitors hissed.

And Sahim woke.

With a howl, the yellow genie shot up from his hammock just as Karim's fingers closed around his ring. "Ahhh! What is this?" Sahim bellowed. He shook his head so hard that the spiders and scorpions scattered from his turban.

Sahim's yellow fingers reached for his ear, which Karim was dangling from like a blue gemstone.

"Karim, you miserable pip of a grape—that can only be you!" Sahim boomed, while Karim wriggled like an eel to avoid his fingers. "Just you wait! I shall crack you open like a bug!"

"We have to help him, Maimun!" Emma screamed. "Or do you want to watch him be crushed? Yallah!" she shouted, grabbing the fringe of the carpet—forgetting in her excite-

ment that she only knew the order for landing. The carpet lurched downward. The dromedary fell over, and Maimun nearly dropped headfirst into a jug. Tristan just managed to catch his trouser leg.

"What are you doing?" Maimun screeched. He pulled Emma's fingers off the carpet and only barely steered the carpet clear of a giant spiderweb. But as he turned it, Sahim's burning eyes were already fixed on them.

"And who do we have here?" he boomed. "The caliph of Barakash delivers his dromedary to me in person. Or did you come to steal my little Sandy Head?"

The dromedary hid its head behind Maimun's back, and Tristan growled so loudly that his entire body trembled.

Emma couldn't take her eyes off Karim, who was still hanging on to his nose ring and trying to pull it off Sahim's earlobe.

"Yes, exactly. That's why I'm here, you thieving sack of mustard!" Maimun screamed as loudly as he could up at the yellow cat eyes. "I am taking it all back, everything you stole from me. And then I will release your prisoners."

"Really?" Sahim growled. His eyes narrowed. He took a breath—and blew them all off the carpet.

I knew it! I shouldn't have opened the bottle, Emma thought as she fell. A sticky spiderweb slowed her fall a little, but she still landed hard on a pile of dusty carpets. Tristan dropped onto her belly. The dromedary landed on its own hump. And Maimun went headfirst into a giant clay jar.

With a nasty grin, Sahim reached for his earlobe again. And this time he managed to grab hold of Karim, despite how hard the blue genie kicked and wriggled.

"Let go of the ring, you bluebird brain!" Sahim growled.

"It is mine!" Karim shouted feebly.

"Let goooo!" Sahim howled. He yanked so hard at Karim's legs that his earlobe stretched like a piece of yellow chewing gum.

Then it happened. Suddenly. The nose ring opened.

Sahim howled and grabbed his ear, but it was too late. Karim was already fixing the ring to his shrunken nose.

And finally he grew.

8

THE BATTLE OF THE GENIES

Karim grew until the giant hall was filled with his blue light. Sahim's palace became cold and damp, and the stuffy air began to smell of spring. The yellow genie trembled like a leaf in a cold wind.

"Finally!" Karim shouted as he stretched his huge limbs.

"Get out of my palace, you inflated hippopotamus!" Sahim screamed. His teeth chattered, and his body grew pale.

"You are the one to leave, Master of Evil!" Karim thundered so loudly that the old walls shook, and the dome above the giant spiderweb started to crack.

Then the blue genie grabbed the yellow genie,

and the yellow genie grabbed the blue genie, and
the two giant genies began to fight.

Sahim's hot skin steamed where Karim's fingers touched it, and soon the spiderweb was full
of little glistening droplets of water. The yellow
genie's movements became slower and clumsier.
One of his scorpions jumped onto Karim's bald
head. It climbed down his nose and stretched its
pincers toward the ring. But Karim just brushed
the scorpion off like an annoying crumb.

Sahim screamed with rage and tried to reach
for Karim's nose ring himself. But his fingers

trembled so badly that he couldn't grab hold of it.

"Are you cold, Master of Evil? You don't like fresh air?" Karim boomed, then he blew his dusky-cool breath into Sahim's face.

The yellow genie shrank back as though Karim had blown icicles into his eyes. He sneezed so hard that his turban slipped. He wheezed as he tried to straighten it again—and then he stared at his hands in shock. They were blue. As blue as the sky above the desert. "Ahhh!" Sahim cried. He stared down at himself. Even his belly was changing color, his ankles, his toes, too. "Oh no!" he howled. "This is abominable. I look like a grape. Like a swamp hen! Like the belly of a bee-eater."

Then he gasped for air, steam shooting from his ears like a kettle, and became as stiff as a rock before dropping into his spiderweb.

"Quick. Stuff him into his bottle, Karim!" Maimun called. His ears were still bright red from falling into that jug.

"Well, that could be a little difficult, oh glory of Barakash!" Karim warbled. He tapped his finger against Sahim's blue nose. "For that he'd have to thaw first, and that might take at least a hundred years."

"A hundred years? That sounds reassuring," Emma muttered. She suddenly felt terribly tired.

Karim leaned down toward her and smiled. "Well, my mistress?" he said. "Are you now happy with my size?"

"Oh yes. I find it quite impressive," Emma answered, smiling back at him. "But could you now free the other prisoners? Believe me, it feels horrible to be locked up in a cage like that."

It took many, many hours to unlock all the cage doors, and the same amount of time again until the last kinglet had fluttered off into the dusky skies and the last dab lizard had slipped back into the desert.

Sahim's palace was quiet. Even the spiders and scorpions had gone.

Only Tristan was still sniffing around the old

walls. The dromedary yawned as it put its head on the sacks Maimun had dragged onto the carpet. "Pomegranates, cactus figs, apricots . . . ," Maimun listed, sitting down on top of the pile. "Tonight there shall be no dry bread eaten in Barakash. Come on, Karim. Let's fly home. The sun's already rising. If we wait any longer, we shall be roasted over the desert."

"Right away, Master!" Karim replied. He

drifted back to the frozen Sahim and pulled the ring off his nose. "A hundred years pass quickly," he said with one final glance at his blue-tinted enemy. "And I've always been a little forgetful."

Emma and Tristan were already sitting on the carpet. Karim leaned down to her and whispered with a broad grin (the grin of a fully grown genie is very, very broad), "Grant me one wish, mistress of my heart! Take this ring into your cold land and have the king of all dogs bury it. I can't think of a safer place."

Emma carefully took the ring from Karim's blue fingers. She still couldn't believe how big they had become. "Of course, with pleasure," she said. "I will tell Tristan to dig a particularly deep hole."

"Wonderful!" Karim called out. "Then let us leave. Oh, I feel wonderful. No genie can challenge Karim the Beardless."

But Maimun carefully cleared his throat. "Aren't you forgetting something, Karim?" he asked. The genie looked at him in confusion.

Maimun crossed his arms. "Didn't you tell me Sandy Head still has three wishes, oh Master of Forgetfulness?"

"Oh, shame on my bald head!" Karim slapped his forehead. "Is there nothing left in this head of mine but desert sand?"

"It's fine," Emma told him. "There's still time. First let us fly back to Barakash. Tristan and I really don't fancy being roasted over the desert."

Tristan confirmed this with a smack of his lips. And so Karim blew the flying carpet with his friends across the wide desert and back to Barakash.

Sahim's palace was quickly covered again in yellow sand.

9

THREE WISHES

For two days and two nights, Emma sat at the beautiful well in Maimun's palace, pondering what she should wish for. She was surrounded by the tame flamingos they had freed from Sahim's cages, and Tristan often came to visit her. But when the third day dawned, Emma still didn't have a last wish. And it was time for her to fly home.

So she went to Karim, who was just then carrying Maimun on his shoulders to the highest tower of the palace. "Karim!" she called. "I give up. I can only think of two wishes. Do you want to hear them?"

"Of course, my mistress!" Karim called back. He carefully put Maimun down behind the tower's battlements. Emma looked into the genie's eyes, which were as black as the night above the sea. She cleared her throat. "Right. My first wish is actually Tristan's," she said. "I don't mind his short legs, but he'd like to be taller, because of the other dogs, and so . . . do you understand?"

Karim nodded. He put his hands together.

"So be it!" he called out, so loudly that all over Barakash the lizards fell off the walls.

Blue smoke rose around Tristan, and when he and his wagging tail reappeared, his legs really had grown longer. And his head had somehow gotten bigger, too. Emma thought he looked altogether a little strange, but Tristan seemed very happy, and he went to give Karim's blue fingers an approving lick.

"Wonderful," said Emma. She cleared her throat once more. "Then here is my second wish. . . ."

"I'm listening!" Karim breathed.

"I wish that my brothers get an itchy scalp for three days every time they annoy me."

"Three days! That's harsh!" Maimun laughed. "I'm glad I don't have a sister."

But Karim just put his huge blue hands together again and called, "So be it!"

A cool breeze brushed through the hot air of Barakash, and a few wisps of blue smoke drifted past Emma's nose.

"Right!" Emma said, while Tristan admiringly sniffed his long legs. "I should get home. After all, I want to see whether my second wish will also work. But I will miss the good weather."

"And we will miss you, too, pasty face," Maimun said, tugging at Emma's sandy hair. Then he whispered something into Karim's huge blue ear.

The genie raised his eyebrows and smiled. "A good idea!" he whispered. He got up and crossed his arms as he looked down at Emma.

"Since you don't have a third wish, oh

mistress of my heart . . . ," he began. His voice sounded so deep and rich that it felt like a warm wind brushing over Emma's face. "My caliph suggested I give you a gift. Something very rare, very precious . . ."

"P-precious?" Emma stammered. "If you're thinking of jewels or something, I really wouldn't know what to do with them."

Karim smiled and clicked his tongue twice. Then he reached into the air as though trying to pluck a bird from the sky. He leaned back down to Emma and held out his hand to her.

On it lay a bottle, barely bigger than a yogurt pot. Emma could see a tiny figure behind the pale-green glass. It was as blue as Karim. "This is a young genie," Maimun explained. "Barely seven years old, but genies grow fast. Come next year you'll have to get him a bigger bottle."

"Oh!" Emma said. She stared reverently through the green glass.

The tiny genie gave her a shy smile and bowed.

"What is his name?" Emma whispered.

"He is called Khalil!" Karim answered. "Which means 'good friend' in your language."

Emma felt a little weak with happiness. "I hope he's not afraid of dogs," she said. Khalil was curiously pressing his nose against the glass.

"Ooh, no!" Karim laughed. "But the cold weather in your land might give him some trouble. You should get him something warmer to wear. It's exactly ten days until he'll slip out of his bottle for the first time. Always pay attention to his color. As long as he's dark blue, he's doing well."

The tiny genie yawned and scratched himself behind one ear.

"He shouldn't really do magic more than

once a day for the next two years," Maimun added. "And you should put him in moonlight every now and then. It'll make him grow faster."

"I'll do that," Emma answered. She held the bottle in front of Tristan's nose.

Khalil looked a little alarmed, but he tried hard not to show his fear.

"Don't worry, Tristan will protect you," Emma whispered at the bottle. "My home is really quite nice, except for the weather and my four brothers. But they can be nice, too, sometimes."

Then she said goodbye to Maimun and the dromedary and the blue-patterned grandmother, who even packed some honeyed dates for her, and Karim took Emma and Tristan home. This time they didn't need a carpet. Karim carried them in his big blue hands.

They landed on the beach just as the sun rose.

And it was almost a little warm.